KINGS & KINGDOMS 3

Y. AKHILESH

Copyright © Y. Akhilesh
All Rights Reserved.

Contents

I
Feel The Fear

Intro: Morningstar thought that he stopped creating the clone of him by killing all the black order, but there was still one member of the black order remaining. She wasBaba Yaga. Baba Yaga created the clone of Captain Morningstar and named it "Antichrist" also known as "Son of Satan."

Summary: Morningstar was wounded and on his knees. Maledictus was also damged. Kraken was not present at the place. Morningstar rises his hand and summons his trident. He threw a big wave of water on all sides. The person attacking him was invisible. He doesn't know if there is someone present or not, but someone was trying to hurt him or kill him. His trident was also not enough to kill the person.

Posieden's Trident [IMAGINARY]

Morningstar calls the Kraken. Kraken comes from below the water and roars. Kraken starts to attack randomly in the air. Morningstar was not with his crew cause he was traveling with Maledictus and Kraken he refused to have a crew with him.

Maledictus Navis [IMAGINARY]

Morningstar knew that Kraken could see the man because Kraken was created by Diana. Kraken was pulled down to the sea. Morningstar stares at the sea. After 15 seconds he starts to see bubbles at a certain part of the sea. He starts to see the place where bubbles were coming and then Kraken comes up. But Kraken was not alive. It was dead and a person with wings on his back was holding it with one hand. The man uncovers himself and says "I am the Antichrist The Son Of Satan." Morningstar could not remove his eyes from him. He was having ten billion questions in his mind. Who is this guy? what is this guy? why does he looks like me? why he has wings on his back? how did he kill Kraken? How can he lift Kraken with his one hand, Kraken is 1,800KG [or] 3000 Pounds? and he was thinking many questions in his mind. Morningstar jumped down the ship and said Maledictus to go far away. Morningstar tried to attack Antichrist, but Antichrist threw Kraken and punched Morningstar so hard that he fell 7 meters away from the place and went 5 meters down into the sea. Antichrist came near Morningstar and said, " I can't feel the fear in you..." Morningstar says "I'm fearless" then he replies, "You are gonna fear soon..." and flies away. Morningstar summons his trident and flies to Kraken. Kraken was dead. Morningstar cries... not loud but he was sad. All the fishes nearby were coming near him and were swimming around Kraken. Morningstar raises his trident up and hits the trident on the ground. saying "Hail Posieden!!!" a blue ray from the top of the sky falls on him and all the fishes start to come near him and he was able to control things underwater. Here Antichrist sees the blue and says "I knew it's gonna happen. You have mastered controlling underwater!!! but it isn't an upper hand for you Morningstar. Now you're gonna **Feel The Fear.**

Kraken [IMAGINARY]

Antichrist [IMAGINARY]

II
Feeling Fear

Morningstar tells Kraken to rest cause it was badly damaged. Morningstar swam 125km and reached the land. Morningstar swimming for 62 and half hours. Morningstar kept walking and after traveling 30km he swam for 10km more. He finally reached Dark Morning. Here all the guards were alert. All were female guards. All aimed their bows, cannons, and guns at Morningstar. But when they saw Morningstar's face clearly they rushed towards him and took him to the watch tower. After a few hours, Morningstar woke up and saw Nikhitha in front of him.

Nikhitha Morningstar [IMAGINARY]

Nikhitha told "what do you want father? any important work?" Morningstar caught Nikhitha's collar and said "Where is Chaos Blade?" Nikhitha raised her hand and summoned the Blade and said "It's with me... but do you ask for it?" Morningstar told "Antichrist is here. he is gonna make us **Feel Fear.** He took me to his knees before revealing his identity. We failed... we didn't stop the black order from making clones of me." Nikhitha said "No!!!! it can't be... Chaos blade is with me and Chaos blade is needed to make the clone." Morningstar stayed silent... and was thinking... then he told "call Atlas."

Chaos Blade [IMAGINARY]

III

Few Younglings

Nikhitha says "Father I have few people for our team to defeat Antichrist." Morningstar says Nikhitha to bring them in front of him. Nikhitha brings a few members in front of him. there were 5 people in that group. All were from Maurya Empire. Nikhitha started to introduce them one by one. The first member was Thaman, the mighty warrior from Ceecave. He had knowledge of the plants.

Thaman [IMAGINARY]

Second is Nihal Rao, Son of Ex-knight of Nikhitha. He has super durability.

Nihal Rao [IMAGINARY]

The third is Gauthami, A female warrior with no one left for her who took a decision to fight. She was Dark Morning's most intelligent human ever. And she never

Feels The Fear.

Gauthami [IMAGINARY]

Fourth is Sarika, A girl who was interested in fighting a war and has extreme knowledge of every type of weapon.

Sarika [IMAGINARY]

Fifth and last was Nishu, A mighty warrior, and great mentalist. He is the strongest Illusionist and Magician in the Orb. He tortures people with tension. He has knowledge of all 4 Vedasof Hindu mythology. He read Quaran, Bible, and Bagavathgita. He has mastered control of every type of weapon and is able to kill a man with dirt. He is young but super strong. Nikhitha as soon as she introduces him says to Morningstar that Nishu is her son.

Nishu Morningstar [IMAGINARY]

IV

The Plan

Morningstar told that Nishu isn't eligible to fight, then Nishu rises and catches the collar of Morningstar saying "Who are you to tell, I am a Morningstar, and people from the family of Morningstars are never unworthy." Nikhitha slaps Nishu and says "He is Capt. Morningstar"All five members including Nishu kneel in front of Morningstar. Morningstar tells Nishu to get up and excuses him for catching his collar.

Nishu Amica Morningstar [IMAGINARY]

Nishu says "You are my hero... Mother told me about you for the last few years. Can you tell me who is your hero, Sir?" Morningstar says "First of all you should call me Grandfather not sir and If you talk about my hero It will be only one for years. Maharaj Chhatrapati Shivaji." Nishu smiles and all from there walk out of the room. After 2 days Atlas sends a reply saying Morningstar to meet him at Collins Mountain. Morningstar takes his new team and sails toward Atlas. It took them only an hour because of Brown Logs. Nishu says "You have so many ships. Don't you grandpa?" Morningstar smiles and says "I own Brown Woods, Brown Logs, Maledictus." Nishu says that he wants to gift him a few ships, but Morningstar declines. [A few moments later.] Atlas asks and says "I have heard of Baba Yaga being seen in the swamps by few people. She is the only possible witch to do so." Morningstar says that they should go towards the swamps. He makes a plan for Atlas, Nikhitha, and Morningstar himself to go towards Apex and Alex for help, and Nishu with his group go towards the swamps.

Swamps [IMAGINARY]

Morningstar on his journey [IMAGINARY]

Morningstar starts his journey. After a few minutes, his ship stops. There were waves, but still, the boat wasn't moving. Morningstar says "What is this?" then Baba Yaga comes out of the sea, flying in the sky. She says **"Feel The Fear."**

V

21,600 Years Prayer

Morningstar takes his trident and flies on Baba Yaga. Baba Yaga knocks Morningstar off. Nikhitha summons Chaos Blade and attacks Baba Yaga. All were weak in front of her. Morningstar wakes up and picks up his trident. He sits and turns upside down. He was levitating in the sky and he goes down into the sea. All were thinking about what is he doing. Baba Yaga says"It's impossible for him to do so. He will fail, but I like that he atlat attempted it." Nikhitha keeps attacking Baba Yaga, but there was no use. After 2 hours of fighting Nikhitha comes to her knees. Nikhitha points her sword at Baba Yaga and says "If you will not leave us that I will use my D&K method [D&K is a method or power of Chaos Blade of killing an enemy but sacrificing him or herself.]

Chaos Blade [IMAGINARY]

Baba Yaga catches Atlas hostage and says "If you kill me then he will also end up dying cause you need to point your blade at the victim." Then Morningstar yells "Don't touch my son" and strikes big lighting on Baba Yaga. Baba Yaga says "You are great!! you meditated for 21,600 years. You meditated in the Aeather dimension which made you gain more of your own strength. You meditated for 120 min which is equal to 21,600 years. I heard that you feel 25 times pain and It's wonderful that you starved for 21,600 years. I will return and will make you **Feel The Fear.**

Baba Yaga, The Witch

VI

At West Sight

Morningstar helps Atlas and first aids him. Atlas says "So, Now you are 21,600+ years old am around 25-35. You and I have a massive difference of 21,000+ years. Isn't it funny?" Morningstar smiles and says "Yes it's funny." Nikhitha and Atlas were not fully healed but they finally reached West sight. Morningstar went to the palace. Apex said "What happened?" then Morningstar said that he want to talk privately. Apex says all to leave the room. Morningstar says the whole story of how Antichrist was born and all the stuff he did. He told everything and he also told the plan to kill him." Apex said "How can we kill him if he can't be killed? Even Posieden's trident and Chaos Blade couldn't kill him." Morningstar says "He may be immortal like me and not feel 25times pain, but he can feel pain and I know how to make him **Feel The Fear.** Let's go to the coast and find ourselves a few ships." After a few moments, Morningstar reaches the port. It is called "Craftships."

Part of Craftship [IMAGINARY]

Craftships is the orb's biggest and best ship manufacturing place. Morningstar says Apex "I want to meet the best shipbuilder." Apex presents an old man named Jarvis May Lent as the best shipbuilder.

Jarvis May Lent [IMAGINARY]

Jarvis catches the legs of Morningstar and says "You are my hero!! Dane killed my son, grandson, niece, and wife. You are the one who saved us. It's my pleasure to help you, sir. I know how to make a ship faster than Brown Logs and

Brown Woods. I want one week's time sir. I will present them as a gift. Morningstar says that one week is the lesser time he expected to give. He thought to give 3 months time to him. Morningstar leaves West sight and goes towards an island called Terra Vini. Where Alex likes to hide a lot and is also a home for him.

Terra Vini [IMAGINARY]

VII
Wine Is Life

Morningstar reaches Terra Vini and as soon as he lands a man offers him a glass of wine. Alex comes and says "Hi father. It's been a long time since saw you. This is my own island called Terra Vini. You will find 10,000+ types of wine. Wine is life for me. It is with me forever. When I am sad I drink it, When I am happy I drink it and when I am nervous I drink it.

Wine

I run a bar here. It extends for 200 meters on both sides. It is the biggest bar in this orb." Morningstar says that he needs help to defeat Antichrist and make him **Feel The Fear**. He explains the whole story to Alex and after listening to that he killed Kraken, Alex drops his wine glass. Alex says that he has a crew, but not strong. Morningstar says okay for his crew and they both went back home. Here Nishu was feeling proud to lead a team. They finally reached the swamps. All of them started to search for Baba Yaga. Nishu says "it's better to be in a team. Do not spit into halves." Nishu and his team saw a hut. They all walked into it. Suddenly a girl from the back attacks Nishu and knocks him. All of them attacked him, but she knocked on them too. Nishu rises and attacks Her. She kicks him and says "You are puny and weak." Nishu wakes up and pulls his pocket dagger out and says "I am a Morningstar and people from the family of Morningstar aren't weak." The girl says "Who are you? how are you a Morningstar? I didn't see you in my life." Nishu says "I am the son of Queen Nikhitha." The girl replies and says "I am Alice Gen Morningstar, Daughter of Atlas Ben Morningstar and Grand-Daughter of Morningstar."

Alice Gen Morningstar [IMAGINARY]

VIII
Alice Gen Morningstar

Nishu says "You are too young and you defeated my team. You are like insane." Alice says "I am quite good at fighting." Sarika comes near Nishu and whispers in his ears saying "She is using a mace and chain. It's the hardest weapon to use." "For what work did you come to the swamps?" asked Alice. Nishu says that they are in search of Baba Yaga. Alice says "I am searching for her and I fought with her too. It was difficult to fight my curse and at last, I got defeated, but was able to escape."Nishu says "Curse!!! what curse?" "Baba Yaga told me that I am weak and she gave me a curse. She made my Anxiety disorder in half. I have fear of sharp objects and blood. Baba Yaga made my personality divide into 3 equal halves. One has fear of sharp objects and second have fear of blood and at least third has none. The third one is the most powerful and whenever I **Feel Fear** a lot she awakens. It's called the **Agartha Curse**." says Alice.

Agartha Curse [IMAGIANRY]

Nishu asks "Who are you now ?" then she replies "I am the first one who has fear of sharp objects. It's not like I can't hold sharp objects. When someone keeps a sharp blade at me and scares me a lot then I fear." Nishu says "I didn't understand it, but it's okay." Alice says that Atlas will send a ship for them tomorrow morning and all started to go to the coast.

Sea Coast

IX

The Ships Are Ready

Here Morningstar went back to West sight to receive his ships. he asked Jarvis to show his ships. Jarvis presented 4 ships for him. Which were only designed for Morningstar and other ships for the war. The first ship was Careys.

Careys [IMAGIANRY]

The fastest ship in the orb. It's faster than Brown logs. It is a steam engine like Brown logs and is more powerful than Brown logs. The second was Kargo the ship which can go underwater. It has a capacity of 30 people and has well durability and speed.

Kargo [IMAGINARY]

Third is Black Wood, The most powerful ship after Maledictus. Morningstar was so happy with Jarvis's work. He praised him a lot. The next day all went towards the swamps to pick up Nishu and his team.

Black Wood [IMAGINARY]

X

Illuminati Again!!

Morningstar finally reaches the Swamps and he was confused by seeing Alice there. Atlas said "Before you sent me the letter some people in my kingdom told me that Baba Yaga is on land. I sent Alice to investigate." Morningstar picks them and his next plan was to call the Illuminati. Alice can't say about her curse on Atlas as she was afraid that he will panic a lot when he hears it and will also not allow her to participate in this mission.

Alice Gen Morningtsar [IMAGINARY]

She somehow manages to bring some guts in her and says about that curse to Morningstar. Morningstar says "It's a good curse, Alice. I studied every curse after I got my curse. My curse is called Dolor Curse which is unbreakable.

Dolor Curse [IMAGINARY]

You will get 3 lives. This means you should get killed 3 times and then you are considered to be dead. Don't tell anyone about this."After a few hours. Morningstar finally reaches the Illuminati. He walks in and asks Mason to help. Mason was the leader of the Illuminati and he accepts the proposal of Morningstar. Morningstar says that they need at least 5,000 people in the army from Illuminati.

Illuminati Symbol

At the same time, Morningstar sends a letter to Neo.

XI
Letter To Neo

15th August 1717
Respected King Neo,

I am Capt. Morningstar and I want an army to fight the Antichrist. Baba Yaga created a clone of me and Antichrist's main goal is to conquer the world. Baba Yaga fooled the black order and made them help to create Antichrist. He is too powerful. He killed my Kraken. He is unstoppable. We need all 5 godly weapons to beat him. We have 2 weapons Posieeden's Trident & Chaos Blade. We want your support Neo. We will meet on 17th August at West Sight. We are gonna make Antichrist <u>Feel The Pain</u>...

Your Sincerely
Captain Morningstar...

XII

Feel The Pain...

All were together and were sailing across seas to reach the swamps. Nishu comes near Morningstar and says "When is this battle going to end?" Morningstar says "It's gonna end now and here. That's why I bought an army of 12,000 people. I messaged Antichrist through my Pidgeon "Lux."

Lux Morningstar [IMAGINARY]

I am gonna destroy Antichrist now itself." After a few hours, the Antichrist appears. He was with the Black Order. Antichrist says "Baba Yaga bought them to life by her magic and now they are under my control." Morningstar picks up his trident and flies at Antichrist. Alice jumps on Baba Yaga and fights with her. Nikhitha fights Reece and Atlas and Alex were guiding their team. Baba Yaga says "You are still puny and weak" then Alice cuts her head off with her mace and chain. But her head grows again and Baba Yaga says to her along the same lines "You are puny and weak still." Baba Yaga captures her with her magic. Alice was not able to move. Atlas was not near her to help. Alice was afraid. Here Nikhitha was using her Chaos Blade and was attacking Reece. Reece says "Puny human!!" and slams her onto the ground. Morningstar was fighting in the sky with Antichrist. Antichrist yells "Satan punch" and punches Morningstar's face. Morningstar falls in Ceecave. The antichrist snaps his fingers and then Ceecave gets destroyed. There were no houses or people left there. Morningstar punches Antichrist so hard that a normal human would die, but Antichrist doesn't move a millimeter. Antichrist catches Morningstar's hand and throws him far away. Here Alice was Afraid, she was feared by Baba Yaga. Baba Yaga keeps a knife on her neck and says "This is what you deserve!!" Here Nikhitha was harmed and she came on her knees. Her Chaos blade was far away fallen on the ground. Morningstar was not able to fight the Antichrist. Then Alice gets switched into her 3rd personality. Alice catches Baba Yaga's hand and cuts it off. Baba Yaga yells loudly in pain and then Alice cuts her head off. Nikhitha was above to be get killed, but then Reece gets attacked by Chaos blade from the back. It was Alex. Reece catches Alex and stabs him with his sharp sword. Alex was above to die by that satb in his body. He points his sword at Reece and kills Reece by sacrificing himself. Here Morningstar was in the middle of the ocean. He figures out that this was the same place where Kraken died. Morningstar goes inside the sea. The antichrist keeps searching for Morningstar. He loudly says "I am gonna make you Feel The Fear Morningstar. Come out." Morningstar comes out riding Kraken from the bottom of the sea and attacks on Antichrist. He says "Feel The Pain... Antichrist. You are the son of Satan, but I am The Satan here. I am The Devil of my orb." Antichrist says "You can heal the dead ones?" Morningstar replies "Yes!!! I revived Kraken and now you are gonna die."Antichrist laughs and says "I am an Immortal idiot!!" Morningstar replies "You are getting captured" then Morningstar controls the sea and creates a way to the core. As the land was below the sea, Morningstar could control it with his powers. He catches Antichrist, pierces his trident into his head, and keeps his leg on his back. With the support of the leg, he puts the force and tears Antichrist's wings off. The antichrist wasn't dead, but he falls in large areas extending to the core. Morningstarcloses the way extending to the core. He flies back to the swamps. He sees Alex injured. Alex says "Dad!! Take care of Atlas." and Alex dies...